Cool Mint

Candy Fairies

Cool Mint

HELEN PERELMAN

ILLUSTRATED BY
ERICA-JANE WATERS

SCHOLASTIC INC.

ISBN 978-1-338-36458-3

12 11 10 9 8 7 6 5 4 3 2 1   18 19 20 21 22 23

Printed in the U.S.A.   40

First Scholastic printing, November 2018

Designed by Karin Paprocki
The text of this book was set in Berthold Baskerville Book.

For Nathan, my sweet

Contents

Cool Mint

1

Cool Ride

A cool morning breeze blew through Marshmallow Marsh. Dash, the smallest Mint Fairy in Sugar Valley, was very excited. She had been working on her new sled all year, and now her work was done. Finally the sled was ready to ride. And just in time! Sledding season was about to begin.

Many fairies in Sugar Valley didn't like the cool months as much as Dash. Each season in Sugar Valley had its own special flavors and candies—and Dash loved them all. She was a small fairy with a large appetite!

Dash was happiest during the winter. All the mint candies were grown in the chilly air that swept through Sugar Valley during the wintertime. She enjoyed the refreshing mint scents and the clean white powdered sugar. But for her, the thrill of competing was the sweetest part of the season. She had waited all year for this chance to try out her new sled!

The Marshmallow Run was one of the brightest highlights of the winter for Dash. The sled race was one of the most competitive and challenging races in Sugar Valley. And for the past two years, Dash had won first place. But this year was different. This year Dash wanted to be the fastest fairy in the kingdom—and set a new speed record. No fairy had been able to beat Pep the Mint Fairy's record in years. He had stopped racing now and was one of Princess Lolli's closest advisers. But no one had come close to breaking his record.

Dash had carefully picked the finest candy to make her sled the fastest. While many of her fairy friends had been playing in the fields, she had been hard at work. She was sure that the slick red licorice blades with iced tips and the cool peppermint seat was going to make her new sled ride perfectly. If she was going to break the record this year, she'd need all the help she could get.

Dash looked around. No one else was on the slopes at this early hour. She took a deep breath. The conditions were perfect for her test run. "Here I go," she said.

On her new sled Dash glided down the powdered sugar trail that led into the white marshmallow peaks. It was a tricky and sticky course, but Dash had done the run so many times she knew every turn and dip of the lower part of the Frosted Mountains. She steered her sled easily and sped down the mountain. The iced tips on the sled's blades made all the difference! She was picking up great speed as she neared the bottom of the slope.

When she reached the finish line, she checked her watch. Had she done it? Had she beat the Candy Kingdom record?

"Holy peppermint!" she cried.

Dash couldn't believe how close she was to beating her best time. She had to shave off a few more seconds to break the record, but this was the fastest run she had ever had. Dash grinned. *This year is my year*, she thought happily.

Suddenly a sugar fly landed on her shoulder with a note. Dash recognized the neat handwriting of her friend Raina. Raina was a Gummy Fairy and always followed the rules of the Fairy Code Book. She was a gentle and kind fairy who was also a very good friend.

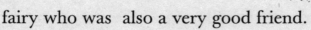

"Raina told you that you'd find me here, huh?" Dash said to the small fly.

The tiny messenger nodded.

Dash opened Raina's note. "She thinks she has to remind me about Sun Dip," Dash said to the fly. She shook her head, smiling.

Sun Dip was a time when all the fairies came together to talk about their day and share their candy. Dash loved the large feast of the day and enjoyed sharing treats with her friends. Now that the weather was turning colder, her mint candies were all coming up from the ground. Peppermint Grove was sprouting peppermint sticks and mint suckers for the winter season.

Dash looked up and saw the sun was still high above the top of the mountains. She had time for a couple more runs. She was so close to beating the record. How could she stop now?

"Tell Raina that I'll be there as soon as I can," Dash told the sugar fly. The tiny fly nodded. Then he flew off toward Gummy Forest to deliver the message.

Flapping her wings, Dash flew back to the top of the slope with her new sled. She had to keep practicing.

My friends will understand, she thought.

As she reached the top of the slope, Dash could think about only one thing. Wouldn't all the fairies be surprised when the smallest Mint Fairy beat the record? Dash couldn't wait to see their faces! And to get the first-place prize! The sweet success of winning the Marshmallow

Run was a large chocolate marshmallow trophy. It was truly a delicious way to mark the sweet victory of winning the race.

With those happy, sweet thoughts in her head, Dash took off. Cool wind on her face felt great as she picked up speed down the mountain. A few more runs and she'd beat the record, sure as sugar.

This year everyone would be talking about Dash—the fastest Mint Fairy ever!

CHAPTER

2

Frosty Sun Dip

Dash flapped her wings quickly, racing toward Red Licorice Lake. She hoped her friends would still be there. She knew that the sun had already dipped below the mountains—and that she was very late. But wait till they heard her great news!

As she neared the sugar beach, Dash saw Raina looking up at the sky. She was pointing toward the Frosted Mountains. "The sun has been down for a long time," she stated. "Soon the stars will be out."

"No sign of Dash?" Melli the Caramel Fairy asked. Squinting, she searched for any sign of her friend.

"Dash has never missed Sun Dip," Cocoa added. The Chocolate Fairy flew up in the sky and scouted the area. "No sign of her."

"Here I am!" Dash called out. Her cheeks were red as she rushed over to her friends. "I know I'm late," she said, starting to explain.

"Let me guess, you were on the slopes?" Berry asked. The Fruit Fairy fluttered her pink wings and settled down on her blanket. "I think all

that time on the other side of Chocolate River is getting to you, Dash. You've never missed a Sun Dip."

"She's all about making the best time for the Marshmallow Run," Melli said, shaking her head.

"She should be concentrating on making the best peppermint sticks instead of a faster sled," Raina mumbled. "Princess Lolli asked Dash to make her two tall peppermint sticks for her new throne in Candy Castle. Did you all know that?" She looked around at her fairy friends. They all looked surprised.

Dash shot Raina a minty glare. "You don't have to talk about me as if I'm not here," she said. "Everything is under control."

The truth was, Dash felt very honored that the ruling fairy princess of Candy Kingdom had asked her to make the sticks for the new throne. When Princess Lolli asked fairies to do something, the fairies all did as she wished. Princess Lolli was a fair and true princess who was very generous and kind. She took good care of the Candy Fairies, and everyone in the valley loved her.

"I don't think Dash has been at Peppermint Grove at all this week," Cocoa said.

"That's not true!" Dash said, flying above her friends. "You don't know the first thing about growing peppermint sticks!"

Melli stepped forward. She didn't like when her friends argued. "Dash, we're just worried about you. It's not like you to miss Sun Dip."

"Or not do as Princess Lolli asks," Cocoa added. "Having peppermint sticks as part of the new throne in Candy Castle is a very big deal."

"That is pretty sweet," Berry said. She turned to Dash. "Have you been working on the peppermint sticks?"

"Yes," Dash said. She landed and planted her feet firmly on the ground.

"How's your new sled?" Melli asked. She sensed that Dash wanted to change the subject—and fast.

"It's *so mint*!" Dash replied with a grin on her face. "I think I have a chance to break Pep's record!" She sat down on Berry's blanket. "How sweet would that be? Today I tied his best time!" Reaching into Berry's basket, she picked a fruit chew and popped it in her mouth.

"Dash!" Berry scolded. "Those chews are not for eating. They're for my necklace that I'm making!" Berry held up a string of sparkled fruit jewels. Berry was very into accessories and never had enough jeweled fruit gems.

"Sorry," Dash said, shrugging. She licked her finger. "It was delicious."

"Did you really tie Pep's record?" Raina asked. "His record has been unbroken for years! No one has even come close to his time."

"Until this year, right, Dash?" Cocoa said.

Dash grinned. "It's all I can think about!"

Raina came over and sat next to Dash on the

blanket. "That's great, Dash," she said. "But you really need to figure out what's going on with your peppermint sticks. Princess Lolli is counting on you."

Melli and Cocoa shared a look. Berry kept her eyes on her fruit-chew necklace.

"You don't understand," Dash said. She looked toward the Frosted Mountains. "This race means everything to me."

"But you have lots of other responsibilities too," Raina said.

"Sorry I missed Sun Dip today," Dash said, getting up. She had just gotten there, but now all she wanted to do was leave. She couldn't stand the look of disappointment on Raina's face.

"Where are you going?" Melli asked.

"Home," Dash said. "I need to frost the tips of the sled again for tomorrow's run."

Raina sank down onto Berry's blanket. "You're not even going to check on the peppermint sticks?"

"I will," Dash assured her friend. "Don't worry."

"But I am worried," Raina said as Dash took off. "I'm very worried."

CHAPTER

3

Champion Race

The next morning, Dash flew out to the Frosted Mountains for another early-morning practice. As she flew over Peppermint Grove, she thought about what her friends had said to her. Maybe they were right. She really hadn't been spending as much time as she should have at the grove. She dipped down to see her peppermint sticks.

The strong, fresh, minty smell of the grove greeted Dash as she drew closer. This was a special place for her. She flew by the tiny mint candy bushes. They were budding new delicious-looking minty treats along the edge of the garden. Farther down the grove she spotted the peppermint sticks that were just starting to push out of the sugar soil.

Looking down the row of peppermint sticks, Dash realized that the sticks could have been bigger. She put her hand on one of the sprout sticks.

"This needs more mint," she said. She walked over to a small shed and got her mint can. She knew peppermint sticks needed lots of mint. Since some of these sticks were for Princess Lolli's new throne, she wanted them to be perfect. Even

though her friends thought she didn't care, she did. "I can race *and* raise peppermint sticks," she declared out loud.

While minting the soil, Dash was distracted. She couldn't stay too long in the grove. She had to keep up with her practice schedule. She sighed. If only her friends understood what breaking the Marshmallow Run record meant to her. Maybe then they wouldn't have given her such a hard time at Sun Dip.

Dash poured more white minty liquid into the ground. Then she gently pulled stray mint weeds from around the sticks and straightened the sugar fence around the grove.

There's no need to panic, Dash thought. She stood back and admired the peppermint stick crop.

Maybe she should spend more time here,

she thought, but she had to get going. A cool, refreshing breeze blew her blond hair and tickled her silver wings. She put her mint can back in the shed and headed toward the slopes. Time for another practice run!

Once Dash was on the slope, she double-checked her sled. Everything looked perfect. Just as she was getting ready to take her first run of the day, she sensed someone standing behind her. She turned to see a Mint Fairy. Dash squinted her eyes. And then her jaw dropped.

"Pep?" she said breathlessly. Her heart was beating extra fast.

The Mint Fairy walked over to Dash. "Yes, I'm Pep," he said. "You must be Dash. I've heard a lot about you."

Dash blushed. "You've . . . you've heard

about me?" she stammered. She could barely speak. Standing in front of her was one of the most famous fairies of all time. And certainly the fastest.

Pep laughed. His teeth were as white as the mint syrup Dash had poured around her peppermint sticks. And his bright green eyes twinkled like the sparks from a mint candy.

"Yes, of course I've heard about you," he said, smiling. "You are about to break my speed record, right?"

"I . . . I . . . Well, I hope to break your record," Dash spat out. She looked down at the packed powered sugar by her feet.

Nodding, Pep grinned. "Princess Lolli says you've got a good chance of beating the record," he told her. He winked. "I had to see you take a run for myself."

"I'm about to go now," Dash said.

"Would you like to race me?" Pep asked. He pulled a green mint sled out from behind a tree. "I'm up for a run. Would that be okay?"

All Dash could do was nod her head up and down. She was too excited to say anything! Racing against the most famous speed-racer fairy was a huge thrill. "Sure," Dash finally managed to say. She pulled her snow goggles down over her eyes and got set to race.

"Sweet!" Pep called out. He jumped on his sled and started to count down. "Three, two, one—GO!"

The two Mint Fairies raced down the slope. They were wing to wing for most of the ride, but when the marshmallow turn came, Pep sped ahead, and he won the race.

"Great race!" he said, lifting up his goggles. "Princess Lolli was right about you."

Dash took off her goggles. "Thank you," she said. "I've been practicing. I really want to beat your speed record. But I have big tracks to fill!"

Pep stood up. "You have an excellent chance," he told her. "I wasn't this fast when I was your age. You need to keep up the practicing. Those last turns through the marshmallow are pretty sticky. But with practice, you can do it."

Dash was so happy that Pep understood her wanting to break the record. "It's so great to talk to you," she said. "My friends don't really understand my racing. They keep after me about my candy duties. They don't get my need to race."

"Well, your friends are right too," Pep explained. He pulled his sled off the slope. "It's great to race, but your first responsibility is your candy crops."

"Have you been talking to my friend Raina?" Dash asked, smiling.

Pep shook his head. "No," he said, laughing. "But if she's after you about tending to your chores, then she is a good friend. A real champion is responsible." He wrapped the rope of his sled around his wrist. "Good luck, Dash. I'll be at the Marshmallow Run cheering you on." He flashed her a smile. "Remember, to be a champion, you have to think like a champion." He gave a wave and turned to leave.

"Thanks!" Dash called out. She was still in shock. As she watched Pep fly away, she thought about what he had told her. She squinted up at the sun. She realized a perfect way to make up with her friends. At Sun Dip tonight, she'd bring some special mint candies for her friends . . . along with an apology. A champion apology!

CHAPTER
4

Sugar Medal Bravery

Since Pep had suggested that Dash practice the turns through Marshmallow Marsh, Dash spent the rest of the day on that part of the run, near the bottom of the slope. She weaved in and out of the turns and tried to shave off extra time. If Pep gave her advice, she was going to take it!

With time for one more full run, Dash was feeling confident. She climbed to the top of the slope for her final run of the day.

This time I can beat Pep's record, she thought. *I can be a champion! I know I can.*

She sat for a minute at the starting line and imagined crossing the finish line below in record time. She closed her eyes and took a deep breath.

Think like a champion! she told herself.

She knew this slope. She could break the old record!

With great sped, Dash went down the mountain. She cleared all the turns and jumps in good time. As she neared the Marshmallow Marsh, she steadied herself. She made a sharp left turn and then a quick right. Then she came around a turn, and something was in her way—something that was not supposed to be in the marsh. Dash steered her sled off the slope to avoid a crash and went straight into a sugar mound on the side of the trail.

"Who's there?" a voice grumbled loudly. "Who's that?"

Dash was startled from her near collision. She tried to catch her breath as she took off her goggles. Then she rubbed her eyes. Was she seeing clearly?

"Holy peppermint," she mumbled.

Standing in front of her was Mogu, the salty old troll from Black Licorice Swamp!

"Who are you?" Mogu growled. He stepped forward and stuck his huge nose down in Dash's face. He sniffed around her. "And what do we have here?" The troll peered down at the tasty sled made of the finest candy.

Dash had to think fast! She knew all about Mogu, who loved candy and stole Candy Fairy treats. He was a sour troll who was full of greed. When Mogu had tried to steal Cocoa's chocolate eggs, her friend had been very brave and strong. Cocoa had even gone to the Black Licorice Swamp on the other side of the Frosted Mountains to get the eggs back! Dash knew she had to be brave as well as clever to get out of this sticky situation. No way was that hungry troll going to get her sled as a snack!

"What do you want?" Dash asked, trying to be

strong. She stood up with her hands on her hips.

"Bah-haaaaaaa!" the troll laughed. "Such a tiny fairy. What are you doing here?"

Trying not to get fired up, Dash did her best to be calm. "The question is, what are *you* doing here," she said. "Marshmallow Marsh is far from Black Licorice Swamp."

Mogu sat down on a fallen tree stump, his big belly spilling over his short pants. He stuck his finger into a soft white mound of marshmallow. "I'm double-dipping today," he said, smirking. "I do love marshmallow." He licked his large thumb. Then he eyed Dash carefully. "But your sled looks very tasty too."

"My sled is not for eating!" Dash snapped.

Mogu laughed even louder. He stood up and waddled over to Dash. His white hair stuck out in a ring around his head. "Oh, I'm not sure about that," he said, licking his lips.

The last thing Dash wanted to do right before the Marshmallow Run was to hand over her new sled to Mogu.

Wrinkling his large nose, Mogu laughed again. "I don't really like mint, but I do enjoy licorice and sugar candies. And I see that is what your sled is made of." He leaned closer to the sled. "And frosted tips. Yum!"

Dash backed away. Mogu's stinky breath was awful!

"Let's make this easy," Mogu said, rubbing his big belly. "You just fly away and leave this for me to nibble on. A marshmallow-dipped sled!" He drummed his fingers on his large belly, and a wide grin appeared on his face.

"This is a very sweet surprise to find here in the marsh."

Staring up at Mogu, Dash couldn't help but notice that many of his teeth were missing. And the ones he had were rotten and black. The troll probably never brushed his teeth.

Dash shivered at the idea of the troll eating her hard work. She didn't want to hand over her sled. But what was she to do? Mogu was much bigger than she was, and much stronger. She looked down at her beautiful, fast sled. She couldn't stand the thought of the sled being a snack for Mogu.

Quickly, Dash tried to think of how Raina would advise her. Maybe she would tell her an encouraging story from the Fairy Code Book? And what about Berry, Cocoa, and Melli? They wouldn't be pushed around by a mean troll. After all, Cocoa even faced Mogu under the Black Licorice Bridge!

The time for sugar medal bravery is definitely now, Dash thought. But she was frozen with fear. The closer Mogu came to her, the more scared she became. What was she going to do? How could she save herself and her sled from Mogu?

CHAPTER

5

A Sticky Situation

Dash knew she was in a very sticky situation. Mogu was growing impatient, and she didn't want to give up her sled to the greedy troll. She could understand his appetite for her sled, but she couldn't let it happen. She had worked too hard on her sled all year to just hand it over to a hungry old troll! Her small silver wings fluttered as she tried to think of a plan.

"You're a Mint Fairy, aren't you?" Mogu said, sniffing around her. A sly grin spread across his face. "You almost smell good enough to eat."

Dash flew straight up in the air. Mogu reached up and grabbed her leg. "Where do you think you're going?" he grumbled. "I'm not letting you out of my sight!" He pulled Dash down and looked her in the eye. "What's a Mint Fairy like you doing in Marshmallow Marsh, anyway?"

"I'm practicing for the Marshmallow Run," Dash said, breaking free of the troll's grasp. "The race is in two weeks."

"Ah, silly fairy races," Mogu said, waving his hand. "A waste of good candy, that's what I say."

Dash didn't expect Mogu to understand about the race. She stood closer to her sled. She didn't like how the troll was eyeing her prized possession.

"Candy is pretty sparse this time of year," he went on. "Maybe it's because you Mint Fairies are so small. I saw those tiny peppermint sticks in the grove. Those are yours? The tiny ones? Tiny candies for tiny fairies!" Mogu leaned his head back and hooted a large belly laugh. "Oh, I make myself chuckle," he said happily.

Trying to keep her cool, Dash took a deep breath. Her minty nature made her want to lash out at the mean troll, but she knew that wasn't the answer. Her mint candies were the sweetest in Sugar Valley. She had to keep focused on the task at hand. If she was going to outsmart this troll, she had to be clever and calm. Her only chance was to try to trick Mogu. She looked up to the Frosted Mountains, and suddenly she had an idea.

"You know," Dash said, "the Marshmallow Run is the hardest race in Sugar Valley. Only a few fairies take the challenge." She watched Mogu's reaction.

"Oh, please," Mogu said. He waved his chocolate-stained hand in front of his face. "I slide up and down the Frosted Mountains all the time. What's so hard about that?" He shook his head. "And I don't even use a silly sled," he added.

"Well," Dash said slowly, "how about you and I race?" She looked right into Mogu's dark, beady eyes.

"Me race you?" Mogu spat. "Oh, that's a good one," he bellowed. "*Baaa-haaaaa!!*" He hit his hand on his knee and continued to laugh. "You are no match for me. You're a tiny Mint Fairy."

So far he was taking the bait. Dash hoped that she could get the troll up on the slope. She stepped closer to the troll. "Yes, a race," Dash told him. "Just the two of us. And the winner gets to keep this sled." She stepped away from the sled, showing off all the delicious candy.

Mogu raised his bushy eyebrows.

"You could have this sled to race," Dash continued, and then sadly added, "or to eat."

Mogu tapped his thick finger on his chin. "Why should I race you when I can just eat the sled now?"

"I've been the fastest fairy on this slope for the past two years," Dash stated. "You don't think you can beat me?"

Mogu smiled. "Beat you?" the troll asked. "Why, you silly little fairy, of course I can beat you. I'm much bigger and faster." He gazed up at the trail zigzagging down the mountain. Then he looked over at Dash. "Nothing makes me happier than taking candy from a fairy. This will be fun. Let's race."

"Oh, it will be lots of fun," Dash mumbled.

Dash knew the slope was narrow and curvy. Without a sled the troll would have a hard time sliding down. But greed made Mogu answer quickly, and soon they were both up at the starting line.

"Are you ready?" Dash asked, looking over at the troll.

"Let's get this going already," Mogu spat out. "I'm hungry, and that sled of yours is looking delicious." He licked his lips as he looked at Dash's sled.

Dash cringed at the way Mogu was staring at her and her sled. There was no room for mistakes here. She had to keep steady and cross the finish line first. Everything was depending on this run.

"Three, two, one, GO!" Dash cried. She took a running start and jumped on her sled. As she rounded the first turn, Mogu was right next to her. He was laughing as he slid along on his large bottom.

"Oh, this is fun," he yelped as he slid along. "I can't wait for my snack at the bottom!"

Dash knew that there was a sharp turn up ahead, and that she had to reach that turn before Mogu. If she took the lead there, she'd be in

good shape to win. Mogu didn't realize the trail curved down the mountain. She was sure Mogu never went near the slope. He probably only slid down the open part of the mountain.

With great skill Dash took the turn, and the lead. Down the slope she went, gaining more and more speed. Glancing behind her, she saw Mogu struggling to stay on course.

"Ouch, ouch!" Mogu grunted as he squeezed himself through the narrow turn. "What kind of trail is this?"

Dash didn't bother to answer. She just kept going. Trolls cannot be trusted, and she wasn't about to wait around at the end to gloat about her win. She had to cross the finish line and get away as fast as she could. Trolls can't fly, and that was Dash's only way out. She just had to be far enough ahead of Mogu to be out of his reach.

The finish line was up ahead, and Dash could hear Mogu huffing and puffing behind her. On the final turn Dash picked up more speed and crossed the finish line. She had no idea if that run broke Pep's record or not. All that mattered was that she had beaten Mogu!

She lifted her sled up and waved at Mogu.

"Sorry, Mogu!" she called safely from the air. "You've been beaten by the tiniest fairy in Sugar Valley."

"*Argh!*" Mogu bellowed as he came to the finish line. He stayed on his back and looked up in the sky at Dash. "Salty sours!" he cried. He beat his fist on the ground.

Dash couldn't help but grin as she saw the

large troll lying on his back. She flew quickly back to Peppermint Grove. Now more than ever she had lots to prove. She wanted to break the speed record, but also prove Mogu wrong about her candy. She was about to make the best peppermint sticks Candy Kingdom had ever seen.

CHAPTER 6

Too Fast

The fresh scent of peppermint put a smile on Dash's face. She was so happy to be back in Peppermint Grove, far from Mogu. She still couldn't believe that she had challenged the troll to a race and won. Wait until her friends heard about her latest adventure!

Feeling lucky, Dash shined up her sled blades

50

with some fresh mint syrup. When her sled sparkled, she took the extra syrup over to the mint bushes at the far end of Peppermint Grove. She poured the white liquid on the branches. She took a deep breath, enjoying the magical moment of creating mint.

The tiny mint buds on the bushes glistened in the afternoon sun. Dash thought about how the crop of tiny mints would soon go to Candy Castle. At the castle fairies from all parts of the kingdom could use the flavoring in their own candies. Chocolate mint, sucking candies, and chewing gum all needed mint. Dash hummed happily as she tended to the her crops.

As she worked, Dash thought about what Mogu had said to her. "Salty old troll," Dash mumbled as she weaved her way through the peppermint sticks. Even though she was small, she could still make the best peppermint sticks in Sugar Valley. "You can be sure as sugar!" she grumbled.

A breeze blew her wings, and Dash noticed the sun getting closer to the top of the Frosted Mountains. She grabbed her bag and filled the sack with some fresh mint treats for her friends. She didn't want to be late for Sun Dip again today.

High above Red Licorice Lake, Dash spotted her friends. She was surprised to see all of them there. Was she late? Berry was never on time for Sun Dip. The Fruit Fairy was always the last one to arrive because she took her sweet time getting ready. Dash wondered what the special occasion was for them all to be there early.

"Hello!" Dash greeted the four fairies. They

were all huddled together and didn't see Dash flying in. "You are not going to believe what happened to me today!"

"Oh, Dash," Melli burst out, racing toward her. "Are you all right?"

"Maybe you want to sit down?" Raina asked.

Berry and Cocoa rushed to her side and spread a blanket on the red sugar sand.

"What's going on?" Dash asked, looking at her friends. "What's with the special treatment?"

The fairies all looked at one another. Raina put a hand on Dash's back. "We've heard about the race with Mogu."

"The sugar flies were all buzzing about the news," Berry told her.

"It must have been awful," Melli said, shuddering.

"Were you scared?" Raina asked.

"Wasn't he salty?" Cocoa added, wrinkling her nose.

Dash was a little disappointed that she didn't get to tell her friends about the race with Mogu herself. Those sugar flies were handy for getting messages to friends, but they could spread a story faster than mint spreads on chocolate.

"I'm fine," Dash said. She flew up fast from the blanket. "In fact, I'm great!"

Melli raised her eyebrows. She pushed Cocoa toward Dash.

"He's a tricky one, that Mogu," Cocoa said slowly. "Tell us what happened. Did he challenge you to a race?"

"No," Dash said. She put her hands on her hips. "Is that what the sugar flies told you?"

The fairies all nodded their heads at the same time.

"Yes," Raina said. "They said that he challenged you, but that you won."

"Well, at least the flies got that part of the story right," Dash said. She sat down on a nearby licorice rock. "He wanted to eat my sled. Can you believe that? I had to think fast and come up with a way to get away from him. Challenging him to a race was the only way."

"And the best way," Berry said with a smile. "You outsmarted Mogu! Well done, Dash."

"He said some mean things about mint candies and Mint Fairies," Dash reported. She looked down at her feet.

"He's just a bitter troll," Raina explained. "You shouldn't let his sour words get to you."

"That's right," Berry said. "He's just grumpy."

"Maybe if he didn't go around stealing candy and being so mean, he'd be happier," Melli added.

"Maybe," Dash said. She stood up. "But I want to prove him wrong. The peppermint sticks are going to be extra-tall this year. Princess Lolli wanted a special throne, and she's going to get a supercool minty one!"

"But what about the Marshmallow Run?" Cocoa asked.

"Oh, I can do that too," Dash said. "I have everything under control."

"We've heard that before," Raina said. She had a concerned look on her face. "We could help tend to the peppermint sticks or help you train for the race." She came up beside Dash and put her arm around her friend.

"I can do it," Dash told her. "I might be small, but I can handle this."

"No one said anything about you being small," Berry pointed out. "You just have a lot going on, and we want to help."

"You told me that I wasn't paying attention to my candy," Dash said. "And now I am. I thought you'd be happy." She picked up her bag. "I have to get back to the grove and then do some wing stretches. I have to be in the best shape possible if I am going to break that speed record." And with a wave, Dash was off.

Her four friends watched as Dash flew back to Peppermint Grove, worried that Dash was moving way too fast—even for a Mint Fairy.

7

Magic Mint

Dash admired the tall and very thick peppermint sticks in Peppermint Grove. She grinned as she squinted up at the beautiful, strong candy. For two weeks Dash had carefully cared for the sticks. Early every morning she would arrive at Peppermint Grove and add more mint to the sugar soil. Her magic touch was working, and the sticks were growing beautifully.

Dash had also kept up with her practice schedule for the big race. In the afternoons she did her workouts and runs down the slope. Sticking to her training program was very important. Dash was one busy Mint Fairy.

Fluttering her silver wings, Dash flew over to the mint bushes along the edge of Peppermint Grove. She checked on the tiny white buds on the thin branches. The mints were ready to pick and send over to Candy Castle. Dash sighed. The Marshmallow Run was tomorrow. She really wanted to get two more practice runs in before Sun Dip today. Once the sun went down, she wouldn't be able to take her run down the slope. She'd have to pick the mints tomorrow. Hopefully as a new speed champion!

"Hello, Dash," a cheery voice called out.

Dash watched as Princess Lolli flew over to her. The beautiful fairy princess was wearing her candy-jeweled tiara and a bright pink dress. Her wings glistened in the winter sun as she settled down on the ground.

"I haven't seen you around this past week," the fairy princess said. She flashed Dash a sweet smile.

"I've been here," Dash explained, "and on the Frosted Mountain slope."

"Ah, yes," the princess said. Her strawberry-blond hair bounced around her shoulders. "Are you ready for the race?"

"Yes," Dash said. "I am."

"I heard about your run-in with Mogu," Princess Lolli said. She stared into Dash's blue eyes. "You were very brave. And your fast thinking to challenge him to a race was very smart."

"I had no choice," Dash told her. "I didn't want that salty troll to eat my sled!"

Princess Lolli laughed. "Well, your quick thinking is a match for your speed on the slope. Well done, Dash."

Dash blushed. She was happy that Princess Lolli had come by to see her. She flapped her wings excitedly. "I'd like to show you how the peppermints for your throne are growing," she said proudly.

Princess Lolli flew beside Dash and saw the tall sticks at the far end of the grove. "Dash, these are wonderful!" she exclaimed. "You have been working hard." She touched the beautiful candies

striped with red and white. "These will make my new throne extra-special. Thank you."

"I'm glad," Dash responded. "Now if I can only beat Pep's speed record. I want to be the fastest fairy in Sugar Valley!"

"There is more to the race than just speed," the princess said kindly. "Skill and quick thinking are needed to conquer that slope. I have a feeling that you are going to do very well this year, Dash. You've already proved yourself to be a real champion. I am very proud of you."

Dash's wings fluttered again. She felt like sailing high about the grove. It wasn't every day that Princess Lolli came to visit with so many compliments. Before Dash could respond, she saw her friends flying toward her.

"Hello, Princess Lolli," Raina called.

"We thought we'd come and see Dash," Berry told the princess.

As her friends flew down to Peppermint Grove, Dash smiled. She was glad to see them.

"I must get back to the castle," Princess Lolli said to all the fairies. "It was good to see you all," she added. "You are good friends to check on Dash. She's been very busy!"

"Bye!" Dash called after the fairy princess. "Thank you again for coming!"

"Wow," Melli sighed as the fairy princess flew off. "Princess Lolli just came by to see you?"

"She must have wanted to see how they are growing." Berry flew up to look over the crop of sticks. "And she must have been very happy to see these." She flew over to Dash. "The sticks are beautiful, Dash."

Raina put her arm around Dash. "I'm sorry we gave you a hard time," she said. "You really have come through for Princess Lolli."

Dash looked at her sparkly silver shoes. "Thanks, Raina," she said softly.

"And we don't want you to feel like you are doing this alone," Cocoa told her. "We know that the other Mint Fairies are busy with their crops, so we've come to help you." A wide grin spread across her face.

"Really?" Dash asked.

Berry laughed. "Sure as sugar!" she exclaimed. "Just tell us what to do. We're here to help!"

"Well," Dash said, walking down the grove's path. "If you are serious, I'd love some help picking the mint candies off the bushes. The candies are ready to go to Candy Castle, but

I wanted to get another practice run in before Sun Dip."

"Licking lollipops!" Berry shouted. "That's easy. We can do that in no time, right?" She turned to smile at her friends.

"Sure as sugar," they all said together.

With five fairies working, the bushes were picked clean quickly. When the baskets of fresh mints were lined up, Dash looked over the crop. "Wow," she said. "I never would have finished this so fast. Thanks for helping me out."

"Can we watch you take a practice run?" Melli asked. "I know you're superfast, but I'd love to get a little sneak peek."

"You bet!" Dash said. "I'd love for you all to come."

The fairy friends all flew to the slope on

the near side of the Frosted Mountains.

"I'm glad that we don't have to fly *over* the mountain," Cocoa said.

Dash could tell that Cocoa was remembering when she had flown to Black Licorice Swamp to face Mogu. "Hopefully, Mogu will stay on his side of the mountain," Cocoa added.

"I bet he is still embarrassed to have lost the race with Dash," Berry added. She folded her arms over her chest. "Serves him right. He should have known better than to challenge Dash!"

"Now let's see how fast you are," Raina said, smiling at Dash.

Dash picked up her sled and headed for the top of the slope. With her friends by her side, there was nothing she couldn't do!

Race Day

The next morning Dash woke up extra-early. She didn't need an alarm to wake her. Today was race day!

Feeling good, Dash glided over Chocolate River. She took a deep breath. The delicious smell of the river filled the air, and Dash watched the rich brown chocolate rush below her. As much as she wanted to stop and have a quick snack, she kept on flying. She had to get to the Frosted Mountains.

Dash was focused on the race! She had checked on her peppermint sticks earlier that morning, and her candies were perfect. Thanks to her friends, she had gotten all her work done. Now she could concentrate on the race—and breaking the speed record.

When Dash saw the starting line banner, her heart began to beat faster. This was the most thrilling time of all!

Carefully, she iced her sled with fresh mint syrup, making the blades glisten in the morning sun. The cold air rushing around her carried the scent of all the winter candy from Sugar Valley. Dash's tummy rumbled. Again she was tempted to stop her work for a snack. But then she looked at her sled. She wanted to finish her task. Very soon the other racers would be there, and she wanted to be done with her race preparations before they arrived.

"Hey there!" Pep cried as he flew up beside Dash. "You are here nice and early!" He flashed her a toothy grin. "I used to love to get to races early too. Nothing beats the calm before the race, huh?"

Dash nodded. She knew that Pep understood. He held out his hand.

"I brought you some mint candies from my garden," he told her. "I hope you like them."

In Pep's hand were three red-, green-, and white-striped candies. They were beautiful. Dash took one and popped the candy into her

mouth. The candy melted away with a burst of mint in the middle. Her eyes grew wide as she tasted the minty flavor. "Yum!" she exclaimed. "These are extraordinary!"

"Thanks," Pep said shyly. "Now that I am not racing as much, I have more time to tend to my garden." He tossed his long hair out of his eyes. "But I wouldn't have traded all that time racing when I was younger. That was a very happy time for me."

"And for me, too!" Dash said, smiling. "I used to love watching you race. That's why I got into racing."

"Well, you are the favorite today," Pep told her. "And we'll all be cheering for you. Remember, take the course slow around that final bend. The marshmallow gets sticky down there."

Dash nodded. She knew just the area that Pep was talking about. "I will," she said. "And thanks for the candy."

As Pep walked away, Dash saw her friends gathered in tight huddle. They came rushing up to her.

"Lickin' lollipops!" Berry exclaimed. "Was that really Pep? He is even sweeter-looking close up! I've only gotten glimpses of him from the sidelines."

"He is supersweet," Dash said, watching him fly off. "He has been giving me good advice."

Cocoa flapped her wings. "That's nice of him. You could break his record today and he still wants to help you out?"

Dash stood back to admire her polished sled. "Well, he'll always hold that record," she said.

"He's the first ever to have gone that fast. I just hope I can prove myself today."

"I think you've already proved yourself," Raina said kindly. "What Mint Fairy ever challenged Mogu to a race and won?"

"While that fairy was growing candy for a royal throne," Cocoa added.

"And won the Marshmallow Run two years in a row," Melli chimed in.

"Soon to be three years in a row," Berry said, laughing.

Dash smiled at her friends. "Thanks," she said. "It means a lot to me to have you here."

"We'll always be here for you," Raina said. She flew over to Dash and gave her a tight squeeze.

Dash made her way to the starting line. There were more racers than ever before. She looked down the lineup of fairies. There were not only Mint Fairies, but all kinds of fairies from around the kingdom. Dash felt nervous. But then she felt Raina's hand on her arm and saw her friends smiling at her. She placed her goggles over her eyes. She was ready to race!

The caramel horn sounded and the race began! Dash quickly took the lead. She knew the race route well. She held the sled's crossbar tightly and steered down the slope. As she took the turn toward Marshmallow Marsh, she checked behind her. No one was there! She was doing great on time. She hunched down low and tried to gain more speed.

On the next turn Dash felt a bump and then noticed that the left blade on her sled was wobbling. She had no choice but to slow the sled down and pull over to the side. She jumped off to examine the sled. Quickly, she saw the problem.

One of the licorice screws that attached the blade to the sled was missing! Dash looked around on the slope for the sticky peg but couldn't spot it anywhere. How could she continue on? Her sled started to wobble more and more. How could she beat the time—or win—with a broken sled? What was she going to do?

A Little Mint

Dash shook her head. Of all the days for a licorice screw to fall out of her sled! This was the most important race! The Marshmallow Run was only once a year. And this was supposed to be her year to break the record. She kicked the ground with her silver boot. Powdered sugar flew all around. This was not how she thought the race would turn out.

What would Pep do? Dash wondered. As she stared at her sled, she remembered that Pep had skidded off the slope in one race. His sled hit a piece of rock candy. He damaged his sled very badly, and he wasn't able to finish the race.

Dash looked over at her sled and thought again. Riding on a broken sled was very dangerous. Her only chance was to fix the sled. And fast.

I built this sled, she thought. *I can fix it!*

Up on the mountain Dash saw the other racers coming down the slope. She had the lead now, but if she couldn't fix her sled quickly . . .

Dash flapped her wings nervously. The cold mountain air was making her shiver. Down the mountain Dash could see a crowd gathering at the finish line. Pep was waiting for her there—and so were her friends. Knowing that she wasn't alone made her feel stronger and gave her a burst of energy.

She put her hands on her hips. In her side pocket she felt a bottle of mint syrup from her morning's work in Peppermint Grove. Holding up the bottle, she thought about how helpful her friends had been the other day. They had given her a hard time earlier, but in the end they were there for her. Just like this mint!

"Holy peppermint!" Dash cried. "That's the answer!" She smiled. "It's worth a try!" she exclaimed. The bright white liquid seemed to glow in the sunlight. She poured the sticky liquid into the hole and stuck the blade back. "Cool

Mint!" Dash said with a smile on her face. The sticky mint held the blade in place!

"Dash! Are you okay?" Raina asked, suddenly appearing by her side. She turned to the other fairies behind her. "See!" she said. "I knew something was wrong."

"What happened?" Cocoa asked. She flew down and put her hand on Dash's shoulder.

Berry and Melli flew down next to Dash. They all had the same worried expression.

"A licorice screw fell out of my sled," Dash said as she flipped it back over. She looked around at her friends' worried expressions. "But I've solved the problem," she said. "Nothing that a little mint couldn't fix!" She tossed Cocoa the bottle of mint. Then she took a running leap and jumped back on her sled.

"Go, Dash!" Cocoa shouted.

"The others are coming," Melli said nervously.

"Don't worry, you have a good lead," Raina said to Dash. She pointed up the mountain to the other racers. "Go! Go! Go!"

"You can do it, Dash!" Berry cheered. "You can make up the time."

"Thanks," Dash said, looking back at her friends. She was glad they had come by to find her. Hearing their encouraging words made her feel stronger. She could still win and beat Pep's time . . . that is, if she got moving! She looked overhead as her friends flew back to the finish line.

She flapped her wings to gain a little more speed. Up ahead was the stickiest part of the

"Due to an unexpected problem on the slope today, Dash was not able to break that record," Princess Lolli continued on.

"Why is she telling everyone that?" Dash whispered to Raina.

"Shhh," Raina said. "Let's see what she's going to say."

"What Dash doesn't know is that she broke another record today," Princess Lolli declared. She smiled kindly at the tiny Mint Fairy and waved her back onto the stage. "Dash, no one has ever won three races in a row. You have set a new record!"

Pep squeezed Dash's shoulders from behind. "I never won three races in a row," Pep said. "When my sled sped off the slope, I wasn't able to think as fast and fix my sled. I lost that year."

He gave Dash a little push. "Go up and get your prize. You deserve it."

"And now you'll be listed in the Fairy Code Book!" Raina exclaimed. "All the record holders are in there."

"*Choc-o-rific*, Dash!" Cocoa shouted.

Berry and Melli hugged Dash and then clapped as their friend flew back up to the stage.

"Well done," Princess Lolli told Dash. She handed her a scroll and a beautifully carved piece of wintergreen mint with gold sugar writing. "We're all proud of you."

"Thank you," Dash said. Her feet lifted off the ground as she fluttered her wings happily.

All her friends gathered around her and gave her a hug.

"Come on," Cocoa said, pulling Dash's hand. "Everyone is heading to Peppermint Grove."

"There's more celebrating to be done!" Berry cheered. She twirled around in her new dress and touched her sparkly fruit-chew barrettes. "Dash, you can't miss the peppermint stick presentation."

In the center of Peppermint Grove, Dash had placed her four peppermint sticks for the fairy princess. The sticks were thick and very tall. Perfect for a new throne!

Princess Lolli was thrilled at the size and color of the sticks. "What a perfect treat," she said. "Thank you, Dash. These are the sticks of a true champion. I will always think of that when I sit on my new throne." She reached out to hug Dash.

The rest of the fairies were busy celebrating.

There was music, and there were lots of mint candies around for the fairies to eat. And Cocoa brought a barrel of dark chocolate chips with fresh white sprinkles for everyone. Berry was right—it was a delicious celebration.

Dash plucked a fresh candy cane from the garden. The candy was sweet and refreshing. A smile spread across her face.

Winter was one of the most magical times in Sugar Valley. And winning was definitely sweeter with good friends and some cool mint.

Helen Perelman enjoys candy from all parts of Sugar Valley, but jelly beans, red licorice, and gummy fish are her favorites. She worked in a children's bookstore and was a children's book editor . . . but, sadly, she never worked in a candy store. She now writes full time in New York City, where she lives with her husband and two daughters.